GROUNDHOG

STAYS UP LATE

To Tom—thanks for inspiring this story —M. C.

To Punxsutawney Phil —J. C.

First published in the United States of America in 2005 by
Walker Publishing Company, Inc.
Distributed to the trade by Holtzbrinck Publishers

For information about permission to reproduce selections
from this book, write to Permissions, Walker & Company,
104 Fifth Avenue, New York, New York 10011.

The artist used gouache on 140-lb. Arches hot press
100 percent rag watercolor paper to create the illustrations
for this book.

Book design by Nicole Gastonguay

Library of Congress Cataloging-in-Publication Data

Cuyler, Margery.
   Groundhog stays up late / Margery Cuyler;
illustrations by Jean Cassels.
   p. cm.
   Summary: Groundhog decides not to hibernate one
winter, even though his friends tell him that he will
become cold, hungry, and lonely.
   ISBN 0-8027-8939-0 (hardcover) — ISBN 0-8027-8940-4
(reinforced)
   [1. Woodchuck—Fiction. 2. Hibernation—Fiction.
3. Forest animals—Fiction.] I. Cassels, Jean, ill. II. Title.

PZ7.C997Gr 2005
[E]—dc21
                                                        2004058273
ISBN-13 978-0-8027-8939-6 (hardcover)
ISBN-13 978-0-8027-8940-2 (reinforced)

Visit Walker & Company's Web site at
www.walkeryoungreaders.com

Printed in Hong Kong

10 9 8 7 6 5 4 3 2 1

GROUNDHOG
STAYS UP LATE

Margery Cuyler ILLUSTRATIONS BY *Jean Cassels*

WALKER & COMPANY ❋ NEW YORK

Groundhog was not the kind of groundhog who liked to hibernate. To him, making a winter burrow was boring. Gathering and storing food was boring. And, most of all, sleeping all winter long was boring.

Instead of preparing for winter, he liked to play hide-and-seek with the rabbits,

possum with the opossums,

and tag with the bumblebees.

"Why do you even bother to hibernate?" chattered Squirrel. "You're never ready when winter comes. You should be looking for nuts and seeds right now."

"I don't think I'll hibernate this year," said Groundhog.

"But you *have* to," said Badger. "How else will you wake up on February second and look at your shadow so we'll know when spring is coming?"

"I don't need to hibernate
to do that," said Groundhog.

Bear shook his shaggy head. "Well, don't
expect us to give you shelter when it snows."

"Or food when you get hungry," said Squirrel.

"Or warmth when you get cold," said Badger.

Finally winter came. Groundhog's friends curled up in their homes for their long winter naps. But not Groundhog. He stayed outside.

Soon it began to snow.

"Wow—snow!" yelled Groundhog. "Time to play!"

Hare ran by. "Want to make a snowman?" asked Groundhog.

"No, silly," said Hare. "I'm racing to my woodpile until the storm's over!"

Weasel ran by. "Want to have a snowball fight?" asked Groundhog.

"Forget it," said Weasel. "I'm scampering to my hole, where it's warm."

Fox ran by. "Want to build a snow fort?" asked Groundhog.

"Not now," said Fox. "I'm running to my den to get dry."

"What a bunch of stick-in-the-muds," said Groundhog.

As the weeks passed, Groundhog built a snowman, threw snowballs at the trees, and made a snow fort.

But Groundhog was getting very hungry. And very thin, which was making him very cold. And most of all, he was getting VERY lonely. So one day, just before Christmas, he padded over to Badger's burrow.

"May I come in?" he called.

Badger opened one eye. "No, I'm too busy sleeping. *Zzzzz.*"

Groundhog scurried to Squirrel's hole.

"Hello, Squirrel," he said. "How about sharing a few nuts?"

Squirrel twitched his tail. "Not now," he said. "I'm taking a nap. Come back in the spring."

Groundhog finally burrowed through the snow to Bear's cave.

"Wake up, Bear. It's me, Groundhog!" he called.

Bear turned over and wiggled one ear.

"Go away!" he growled. "I warned you not to bother me."

Poor Groundhog. So hungry. So cold.
So lonely. All night long he stayed awake.
But that night as he shivered and shook, he
began to get an idea. An idea that would
put food in his belly *and* give him friends
to play with!

A few days later, the sun came out and the snow started
to melt. Groundhog climbed to the top of Hollow Hill and
pointed his nose to the sky. He opened his mouth and yelled:
"Spring's come early! Let's celebrate!"

The animals poked their heads out of their dens. They wriggled out of their burrows. They crawled out of their holes. How wonderful to have an early spring! Even though it was cold and there were patches of snow on the ground, spring was on its way. They gathered the food they had stored in the fall and carried it outside.

Groundhog was waiting for them.

"Happy spring!" he lied. "I didn't see my shadow,
so spring is coming early. Let's eat!"

"Hooray!" yelled Bear. "Hooray!" shouted the other animals. They laid all of their food on a big stump. Groundhog dove into the dried berries and nuts and seeds. Soon everyone was eating and celebrating.

That is . . . until something unexpected started to happen. A snowflake fell from the sky. And then another. And another. Soon the snow was swirling around them like tiny stars.

"I thought spring was coming early this year!" complained Squirrel.

"I'm getting very cold and very tired all of a sudden," moaned Bear.

"I need to take a nap," said Badger.

Squirrel skittered back to his hole and looked at his calendar. It was only *January* second!

"Groundhog played a trick on us!" he yelled.

"It's not February second. Groundhog Day is a whole month away!"

"What a nasty trick!" cried the animals.

"Groundhog should be punished!"

But Groundhog didn't hear them. He was so sleepy after his big
meal that he had crawled into his burrow and had fallen fast asleep.

And he slept and he slept right up until February second,
when his eyes popped open for Groundhog Day.

He stepped out into the fresh air. The snow had melted, the birds were singing, and buttercups dotted the woods with color.

"It's spring!" said Groundhog. But when he looked down at the ground, he saw his shadow. It looked a little strange and it was a funny color, but it had to be his.

"Nuts!" he said. "Six more weeks of winter." And he returned to his burrow and went back to sleep.

The other animals came out of their hiding places.

"Our trick worked," said Badger. "That shadow we painted sure fooled Groundhog!"

While Groundhog slept through spring,
his friends enjoyed the sun warming their fur
and the breezes ruffling through the trees.
But did Groundhog learn his lesson? . . .

NO!